Big Finn and Miss Quinn's
Birthday Party
CATHERINE BEACH

Hello
meet
Big Finn and Miss Quinn

Lily and Lou Lou are two happy giraffes,
who hang out all day and have lots of laughs.
They are very excited about a party today
and are trotting along to find the quickest way.

The party will be fun for the hippo twins,
one named Big Finn and the other Miss Quinn.

Boho the elephant is hurrying along,
dragging the present with her trunk so long.

The ducklings are excited; they are waddling along trying to keep up, they start singing a song!

Mother Duck looks pretty in her bonnet, so blue,
carrying her basket filled with party ragu.

Bruno, the bear came down from the hills,
with his two little cubs called Doby and Gills.

They're off to the party to wrestle and play
and chase the ducklings around all day.

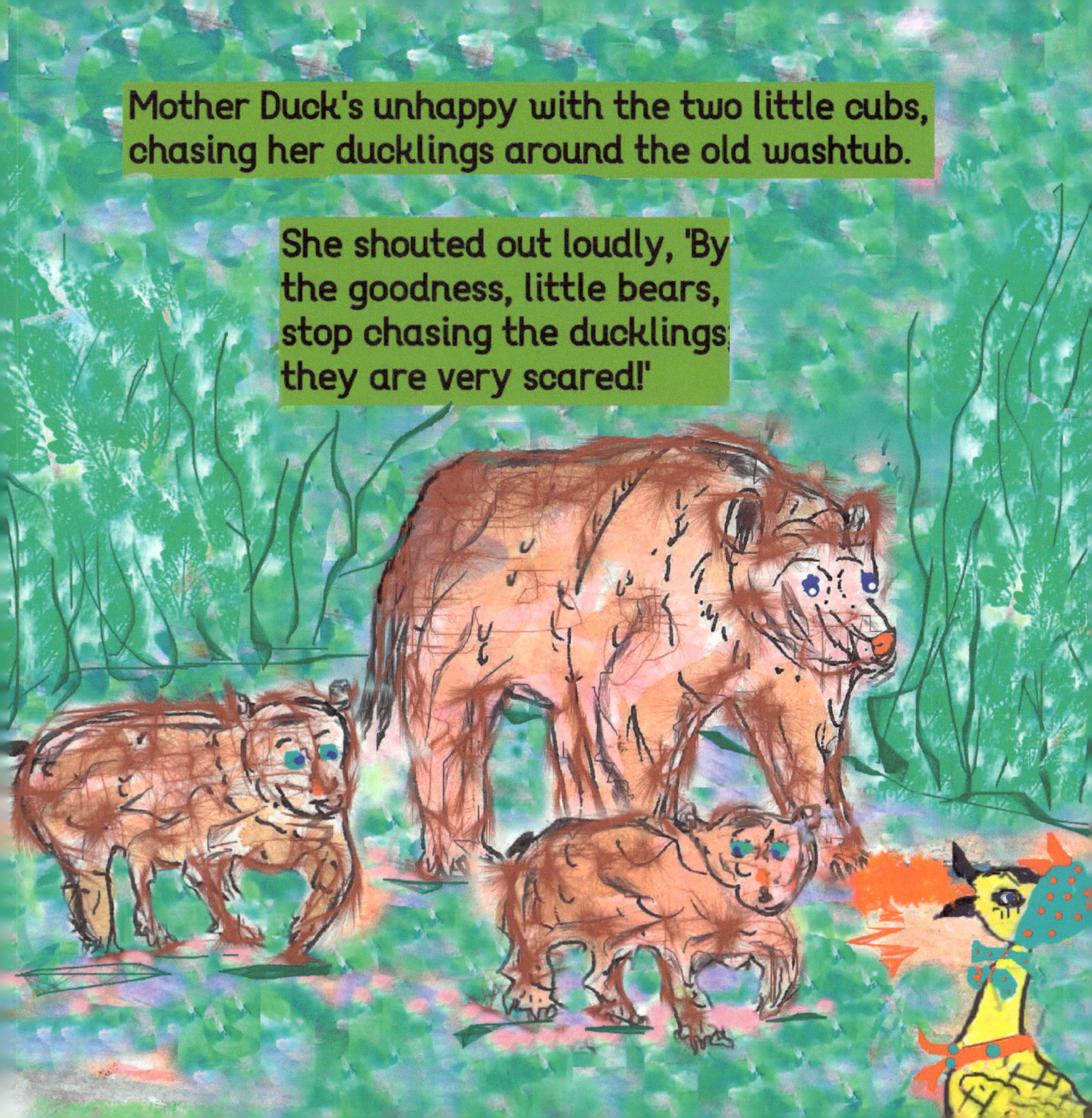

Mother Duck's unhappy with the two little cubs,
chasing her ducklings around the old washtub.

She shouted out loudly, 'By
the goodness, little bears,
stop chasing the ducklings;
they are very scared!'

Pinky the Pig and Daffy the Donkey,
are mucking around and being quite shonky.

They filled up a bucket and thought up some tricks,
and are planning on playing pick-up sticks.

'We are ready to go!'
said Mary the sheep
to her little lamb
called Angelique.

Angelique jumped up and
frolicked about
all ready for the party to
play and hang out.

All the animals join in to sing the Happy Birthday song,
while Big Finn and Miss Quinn dance happily along.

Balloons in the air
and candles on the
cake, they kick up
their heels and
wriggle and shake!

They played Duck, Duck, Goose!
and then Hide 'n' Seek,
Miss Quinn said,
'Cover your eyes and do not peek!'

The pink fairy floss
and raspberry drink
made them so happy
they could not think.

The best party game was
pick-up sticks, and then it
was time for fish and chips.

The air is fresh and the sky very pink
the animals take a moment to stop and think!

So much fun to have good friends;
they can't wait to catch up and party again.

Time to head off and make some tracks,
down the windy road to their wooden shacks.

They are all exhausted after a big day out,
so much to dream and think about.

Did you know
A giraffe's neck is too short to reach the ground.

Goodnight   Sleep Tight

A story to be told

Beads of Paradise welcomes Books for Little Bandits

Catherine Beach is an author and illustrator of Books for Little Bandits

It all started when Catherine moved her city life to the country...all in the name of love. Living on a mixed cropping and sheep farm, surrounded by vast open space and never-ending plains with lively wildlife, Catherine found the pace to be much slower and began to miss the hustle and bustle of city life. This was when she decided to bring her own hustle and bustle to the farm by fulfilling her creative passion.

It began with Beads of Paradise because every day on the farm was like a new day in paradise (well...not always!) Beads of Paradise became her haven. Catherine handcrafted costume jewellery and accessories for brides spanning over a decade. Suddenly, Covid took control, and while there were fewer weddings, there were more babies...

This led Catherine to her next escapade; Books for Little Bandits. Catherine had been spending a lot of time painting, using printmaking and digital techniques in her art, and she has been known to tell a good story or two. Books for Little Bandits is a collection of children's storybooks that combine Catherine's art and storytelling techniques to give families insight into life's adventures in a fun and colourful way.

"All it took was a paintbrush and an idea... and I went for it!" (Catherine)

Who knows what the next story could be about!

Books for Little Bandits

A collection of children's storybooks individually handcrafted using printing techniques, painting and storytelling.

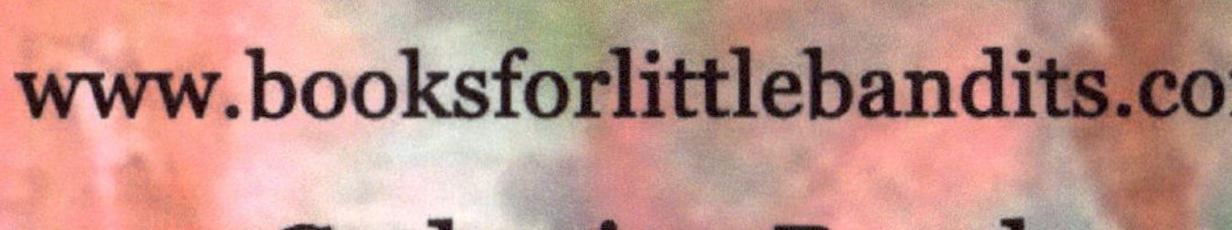

www.booksforlittlebandits.com

Catherine Beach

ISBN 978-0-6455411-0-6